# SOMETHING IN THE AIR

CASE FILES: POCKET-SIZED MURDER MYSTERIES

RACHEL AMPHLETT

# SOMETHING IN THE AIR

# CHAPTER ONE

The passengers for flight Z341 shuffled weary feet across the baking concrete apron leading away from the departure lounge, the air ominous with the stench of ozone and aviation fuel.

Latecomers staggered as they left the cool air-conditioned terminal, assaulted by an unforgiving environment thick with humidity and the roar of aircraft engines.

In the distance, beyond the flat airfield, away from the straggly eucalypt and palm trees that flanked the chain link security fence, a lightning storm flashed and wavered across the fringes of the hinterland.

Most of the passengers carried hand luggage – a backpack, a laptop case, a rollalong suitcase that would be squashed and coerced into the overhead lockers.

Their faces were a mixture of reluctance and resolve, excitement and trepidation depending on whether their destination was the exhausted end of a trip or the start of something new.

The line shuffled forward, urgent now, eager to get away following a forty-minute delay after thunder shook the departure lounge glass and rumbled across Queensland's Sunshine Coast while streaks of lightning scorched the clouds.

Amy gripped the nylon strap of her black backpack, knuckles white.

It had been passed through the security checks before she'd arrived at the airport, then thrust at her in a corner of the departure lounge, away from prying eyes.

Jaw clenched, she stepped sideways from the crocodile line obediently following the zig-zagging yellow lines towards the aircraft.

She watched as a man in a black suit jacket and jeans stared sightlessly from his perch near the top of the steps, his eyes obscured behind sunglasses, his mouth downturned as an indignant screech pierced the humidity.

She shifted her gaze to a man and child

approaching the steel steps leading up to the fuselage.

The toddler was loud and insistent, snatching away her hand from her father's and stretching out to reach up to the rail. The little girl shook her head when the man offered assistance, his arm hovering above her slender shoulders, his face lined with worry.

In front of them, already climbing the steps, was a steady stream of men and women gazing across at the waiting line below with a degree of smugness.

'He should pick her up.'

Amy glanced over her shoulder to see a woman in her mid-sixties glaring at the steps, then turned back and hurried to keep up with the queue, eyeing the boarding pass in her hand.

Seat C3.

Business class.

Near the front, an aisle seat.

Despite what the boarding pass said, despite any hope she would be seated before everyone else, the passengers were being boarded at the same time in an attempt to get the plane off the ground without further delay.

Another five minutes shuffling forward in

the queue, and then Amy climbed the steel staircase – careful not to leave her fingerprints on the rail – and entered the gloom of the cabin, goosebumps sweeping across her bare arms while she blinked to adjust her vision.

She frowned, recalling the seat map that was shown to her at the last minute.

Only one passenger beside her, in seat A.

D and F were on the other side of the cabin.

No B, no E, not until you passed beyond the thick soundproof flame retardant curtains and into the economy cabin.

Just under two hundred seats in total. And almost all of them were full this morning.

All adults, apart from the one little girl farther along in economy, eyes wide with anticipation while her seatbelt was fastened around her.

Amy swallowed.

How many innocent people could be injured or worse by her actions?

Bystanders, the journalists would call them when it was all over.

Collateral damage, said the man who disappeared into the crowded terminal after handing her the bag.

She had lost sight of him within seconds.

'Good morning.' The female flight attendant beamed, flashing perfect teeth amongst impeccable make-up.

Amy forced a smile, handed over her boarding pass even though she could see her allotted place waiting for her, teasing her with its proximity.

Sarah, the woman's name tag pronounced, the brass effect catching in the overhead lights and making Amy blink as she took back the pass.

The same woman who had been working at the departure gate moments before.

The same woman who had allocated her the seat, lips pursed at the last-minute change, eyes worried.

No matter now.

It was too late to turn back.

Turning away, Amy swung her bag from her shoulder and hurried to take her place.

The man in the business jacket and jeans glanced up at her as she approached, his sunglasses perched on top of his head now, green eyes darting to the exit door as she lowered herself into her seat beside him.

He was pale, any semblance of a tan fading beneath the collar of his white shirt while he ran a finger underneath it, blanching as the final passengers boarded.

She ignored him and instead placed her bag under the seat in front of her where she could see it before arranging her long legs and tucking her flowery long skirt around her ankles and fastening her seatbelt.

As she clipped the buckle into place, she spotted her neighbour's boarding card sticking out from the seat pocket in front of him.

*Jed McIntyre.*

Then a man's overstuffed carry-on bag scraped her bare shoulder, and she grimaced, flicking her hand while he apologised before hurrying away.

'You'd have thought he'd have put that in the hold,' murmured the man beside her, his voice unsteady.

'Too much hassle to wait for it at the other end, I suppose. Cairns can be busy at the best of times,' she replied, before eyeing an identical backpack to hers squeezed between his feet. 'Travelling light?'

'This time.' He cleared his throat. 'A last minute trip. You?'

'Something like that.'

CHAPTER TWO

The steady drone of the aircraft's twin engines coalesced with the murmur of passengers' voices as it climbed steadily away from the coast to find its route north.

They had left the storm behind, reaching a cruising altitude of thirty-five thousand feet in a steady banking motion before levelling out.

Amy listened to the regular pings and announcements, the final one a warning to remain seated in case of turbulence as her ears popped with the changing cabin pressure.

Gaps within a soft carpet of tumbling grey and white clouds revealed glimpses of a turquoise coast giving way to darkening waters, and the businessman – Jed, she reminded herself – turned his attention to the window, squinting against the sun's glare.

The colour still hadn't returned to his face, and when Amy lowered her gaze to his hands, she saw he gripped the leather seat rest between them, knuckles white.

She leaned her head back against the seat as he turned away from the view, and closed her eyes for a moment, heart racing.

It wasn't meant to be like this.

Thank God it was a short flight.

Two hours, maybe less if they caught a tailwind.

Her attention snapped back at a low groan from the seat beside her, and she opened her eyes to see the man wiping his forehead with his fingers.

'Are you okay?'

He shook his head, then gave her a rueful smile. 'I'm a nervous flier.'

'Then why…?'

'It was a last minute change of plan. I usually drive up if I'm visiting over a weekend.'

'To Cairns?'

'Like I said, I hate flying.'

'Do you want some water?' Her finger hovered over the call button.

'No, no. That's all right. I don't want to

make a fuss.' He swallowed, forced a smile. 'What's your name?'

'Amy Oliver.'

She bit her lip the moment the words passed her lips.

There was the first lie.

Stupid, she knew.

The more lies you told, the more chances there were of being caught, they'd told her.

She eyed the bag between her feet, the boarding pass tucked inside.

The one with a different name printed across it.

The man held out a hand as she straightened. 'Jed McIntyre.'

'Nice to meet you.' She returned the handshake, his grip weaker than she expected.

'Why are you flying to Cairns, Amy?'

'I'm visiting my parents. I couldn't get a flight at Christmas because I stupidly left it until the last minute, and then I couldn't get time off from work anyway.'

She held her breath, waited for the next inevitable question.

'What do you do?'

And there it was, right on cue.

'I'm a project administrator for an

engineering company. Pipelines, things like that.'

Lie number two.

'It's not very exciting,' she added. 'What about you?'

'I'm a consultant. Self-employed.'

'Oh, doing what?'

His gaze hardened, then a split second later he smiled.

It didn't reach his eyes.

'I suppose you could say I introduce people who are interested in doing business together.'

Amy gestured to the business magazine in his lap, not wishing to push the matter. Not yet. 'An entrepreneur, then?'

The fuselage shook, and her stomach lurched as a woman cried out from the rear of the aircraft.

'Bloody hell,' Jed muttered, his grip tightening on the armrests.

'It always gets turbulent around here, especially after a storm,' said Amy while the pilot's voice filled the cabin, his soothing tone reminding everyone to wear their seatbelts. 'It's nothing to worry about.'

Jed shot her a sideways glance and swallowed. 'You're sure?'

'Absolutely. You should see what it's like on the Brisbane to Newcastle route. I spilt a gin and tonic in my lap on that flight once.'

He managed a chuckle, his hand moving to his shirt collar, loosening a button.

Amy reached into the seat pocket in front of her and retrieved the complimentary paper bag, smoothing its creases. 'Do you want this?'

'Not yet.' Jed gave her a sheepish smile. 'I'm not usually like this.'

'I'll bet. What are you doing when you get to Cairns?'

'Why?'

His smile was gone, a cold glare taking its place.

'Sorry, I didn't mean to be nosy.' She held up her hands to placate him. 'I was just trying to take your mind off the turbulence.'

'No, I'm sorry.' He took a deep breath, the fake smile back now. 'Just catching up with some friends, that's all.'

'Some time out?'

'That's it.' Jed grimaced as the turbulence decreased and a low ping accompanied the seatbelt lights going out. He unclipped his belt. 'Would you mind…?'

'Of course. I think the one this end is

occupied though.' She pointed to the red light above their heads. 'Looks like you'll have to use one of the others.'

Scrambling from her seat, kicking her bag under the one in front so he didn't snag the strap on the way past and reveal its contents, she shuffled forward and watched while he made his way to the toilets at the back of the aircraft.

He grabbed at the back of seats as he walked, his gait unsteadied by the swaying motion of the aircraft while the turbulence dissipated.

Once he had disappeared into one of the cubicles, Amy dropped into her seat, legs shaking.

He hadn't recognised her, she was sure.

CHAPTER THREE
_______________

Amy's fingers clawed at the strap of her backpack as she desperately trying to untangle it from the metal footrest folded up under the seat in front of her.

She gave it a final hard yank and sat back, gasping from the effort before peering over her shoulder.

There was no sign of Jed.

She opened it with a shaking hand, heart racing while she tried to locate her mobile phone amongst the borrowed purse, car keys, leather-bound diary with its empty pages…

Locating it underneath a tangled set of old earbuds and unravelling the wires that snagged around it, she angled the screen so she could read the last text message.

It gave her no comfort.

She was on her own, over five miles up in the air, and in a pressurised cabin.

She thumbed a brief update, then pressed send.

Putting the phone back in the bag, her fingertips brushed against cold steel, and sweat prickled at her brow.

Not yet, she reminded herself.

They said to do it once the aircraft had landed.

Not before.

Just in case.

Swallowing, throat dry, she watched as a teenager exited the toilet, waited until the girl had passed, then signalled to Sarah.

'Can I have some water please?' she asked, shoving the bag back under the seat.

The crew member nodded, her eyes widening before turning away.

'Jesus, the stench coming out of that place.'

Amy jumped at the sound of Jed's voice, then gave a wan smile as he towered over her.

'We've only been in the air forty minutes,' he continued, nodding his thanks as she moved out of his way. 'God knows what it'll be like by the time we land.'

'Here's your water.' Sarah returned, her gaze flitting to Jed. 'Anything for you, sir?'

'I'm fine.' He eyed the small plastic cup in Amy's hand and shook his head. 'I'd be careful how much of that you drink if I were you. I wasn't kidding about the toilet.'

Her choked laughter died on her lips at the sound of the curtain separating them from the economy seats followed by determined tiny footsteps, and then her heart lurched at the small voice beside her.

'Mummy!'

'God, I'm sorry – so sorry.' The child's father placed his hand on his daughter's shoulders, gently peeling her away from Amy's armrest. 'She's been visiting her mum in Maroochydore this weekend... Angela looks just like you from the back... I'm sorry, she was looking for the toilet.'

Amy shook her head, forcing a smile. 'That's fine. It's okay, really.'

He breathed a sigh of embarrassed relief, then grinned at his daughter as he led her away. 'You can use the toilet at the other end, Lizzy. Come on, off we go.'

Turning away from the aisle, Amy drained the last of her water, scrunched up the cup and shoved it in the seat pocket hearing a satisfying crackle as the plastic yielded.

She bit back a sigh, aware that what came

next, what surely had to follow would affect the lives of everyone on board the flight, including the little girl.

Should she stop?

Tell them it was a mistake, that she couldn't bring herself to carry out her mission?

What would be the ramifications when the man at the top found out?

A throaty grunt shook her from her jumbled thoughts.

'They're a handful at that age,' said Jed, shaking his head while he turned his attention back to his magazine, flicking over the page.

'Do you have kids?'

'Two, but they don't live with me.'

'Oh.'

'Trust me, their mother's welcome to them.' He glanced over. 'What about you?'

'Me?'

'Yes. Do you have kids?'

'No.' She rubbed at the skin where the wedding ring used to be and forced a smile. 'Never say never though, right?'

Lie number three.

# CHAPTER FOUR

The conversation died after that, and Amy spent the next forty-five minutes willing the aircraft to reach its destination as soon as possible.

Unknown to the crew, it would be the last flight they would take today.

She just wanted to get it over with now.

End it.

The turbulence returned to shake the cabin from side to side as they skirted past Townsville and Magnetic Island, the pilot's announcement at odds with the bright sunshine that flooded the left-hand side of the aircraft and bathed her ankles with welcome warmth.

Tearing her gaze away from Jed's fingers gripping the seat rest as he stared through the window, she closed her eyes while her thoughts turned to the past two weeks and a past filled with happiness, love and laughter.

Until the last day.

Today.

Why her?

Why now?

'Flight attendants, prepare for landing please.'

Amy grimaced and opened her eyes.

That damn pilot again.

Relaxed, confident, assured.

'I hate this part almost as much as taking off,' Jed muttered, peeling his hand from the leather and flicking through the final pages of his magazine, ignoring all the adverts squashed into the back pages and the flippant opinion column shoehorned onto the last page. 'Never again.'

'No more flights for you?' She couldn't resist a smile when Sarah and her colleagues leapt into action and began a well-practised march along the aisle, safety first and foremost in their minds while she carried *that* in her bag. 'What will you do instead?'

He shrugged. 'I don't know. Depends on the next couple of days, I suppose.'

'Well, whatever it is, I hope it goes well for you,' she lied.

Number four.

'What are you going to do when you get to Cairns?' Jed asked. 'You never said.'

'I haven't thought about it much,' came the easy reply.

Number five.

She cleared her throat. 'Well, actually I have. I thought I might spend the weekend in Port Douglas. I wasn't due back at work until Monday, so...'

'You'll love it there.' He shot her a dazzling grin.

'Do you know it well?'

'I've been there once or twice...' His good humour dissipated, a frown chasing away his smile. 'I'm heading up there myself actually.'

'Oh?'

He gave a slight shrug. 'A mate of mine's got a boat, that's all.'

'Nice. Is it big?'

'Forty-five feet.'

'Wow. Yes, I'd call that big. Where are you going?'

His top lip curled then, and he turned back to the window as the aircraft banked gently to the left, its engines changing tone as another alert beeped in the background while they started to lose altitude.

Amy bit back a curse, her ears popping. 'Sorry, I can't help being nosy sometimes. I...'

*Stop.*

Six lies would be pushing her luck.

And she needed as much of that as possible.

Especially now.

'Cabin crew, prepare for landing.'

'Thank Christ for that.' Jed flapped the magazine closed and tucked it into the elasticated pocket before tightening his seatbelt.

Amy's eyes fell upon the backpack beside his feet, and she chewed her lip.

Beyond the window, sunlight sparkled off the rolling waves chasing towards the Cairns beaches, and then they were banking again, lining up for the steep descent alongside the range of hills bordering the city.

Jed ran a hand across his jawline as they skimmed across car rental lots and eucalypt trees, and swore under his breath as the wheels smacked the tarmac.

Exhaling as the aircraft rapidly braked, Amy willed her heart rate to slow as she watched another aircraft taxiing into place for its departure.

Blood rushed in her ears, dulling Sarah's clipped instructions to passengers over the intercom, the flight attendant keeping a wary eye on the rest of the staff while she explained to passengers that there might be a delay in leaving the aircraft.

'Why?' Jed murmured.

Amy glanced out the window across the aisle to see the runway petering out, and then the aircraft swung left, accelerating forwards.

When she turned back to Jed, his gaze was fixed on a corrugated iron roofed hangar set away towards the perimeter of the airfield.

The doors were open wide, exposing a darkened maw where no light penetrated.

'Something's not right,' he said, twisting in his seat to peer through the reinforced glass. 'We're nowhere near the terminal.'

'What do you mean?' Amy tried to see past him, her skin crawling.

*This isn't what they said would happen.*

She gasped as three federal police vehicles emerged from the hangar at speed and drove straight towards the aircraft.

Gasps and murmurs filtered through the cabin as passengers ignored Sarah's commands and rushed as one to peer through the windows.

Jed turned to face her, his green eyes filled with hatred.

'Shit,' they said in unison.

Then Amy unclipped her seatbelt and lurched for her bag, pulled out a Glock 9mm and aimed it at him.

# CHAPTER FIVE

'Who the hell are you?' Jed snarled, eyeing the weapon hovering under his nose.

The couple in the row opposite cringed away, while a woman behind Amy's seat emitted a shocked scream.

'Amy Cornish.' She moved into the aisle and straightened her shoulders, emboldened by the weight of the gun in her hand. 'Australian Federal Police. Pass me the backpack. Slowly.'

As he bent over to retrieve it, Amy glanced over her shoulder. 'Sarah, I need you to pull the curtains.'

The crew member unbuckled her belt, the metal clasps clanging against her seat while her colleague's mouth formed a perfect "o".

She brushed past Amy, unhooking the

curtains to shield them from the shocked faces of those in the economy section, then scrambled back to her seat, her bright red lipstick a stark contrast to her pale features.

The four remaining passengers in business class flinched when Amy glared at them.

'Stay in your seats. Don't move.'

When she turned back, Jed was holding the backpack against his chest, his gaze fixed on the exit door.

'Don't even think about it. I don't miss, so put the bag on the seat, and then put your hands on your head.'

A sudden jolt rocked the aircraft and she staggered sideways, the gun slipping from her grip.

Shock registered a split second before instinct took over, her body twisting while she fell, her gaze never leaving her target.

Jed pounced, sinews flexing as he lurched towards her, the backpack falling into her seat while his hands grasped at the empty space where she had been standing.

Her elbow clanged against the metal underside of the seat and she stifled a cry, desperately watching the gun's trajectory as it tumbled through the air, slid across the carpet and clattered to a standstill under the crew seats.

She rolled over, started to crawl towards it and then felt a strong hand wrap around her ankle.

Glancing over her shoulder, she saw an evil smile cross Jed's mouth.

'Got you,' he spat.

'Yeah, right.'

She flipped, lashing out with her foot at the same time, and heard the satisfying crunch of cartilage and soft tissue as her shoe found his nose.

He reeled backwards, bellowing.

Amy didn't hang around.

She scrambled towards the Glock, straightened and then planted her feet, her grip rock steady.

Breathing heavily, one hand on the back of a seat while she cursed the sudden braking motion that had nearly ended her life, she watched as Jed tried to stem the flow of blood with his sleeve.

'You bitch,' he hissed.

Amy ignored him and instead tugged the backpack towards her, shaking it to loosen the zip.

It slid open, and she shuffled through the

contents, her fingers caressing the bundles of cash lining the inside.

Then a light blue cotton shirt tumbled out, creased and bloodied.

A driving licence slipped from the breast pocket, an ugly stain obliterating the embossed signature but not the photograph or the details underneath.

She raised an eyebrow. 'What did you say your name was?'

'McIntyre.' His voice was muffled, thickened by blood and pain.

'That's interesting.' Amy flicked the licence around to face him. 'Because the body of a man matching McIntyre's description was found floating off a jetty on the Maroochydore river this morning, his ID missing along with half his face.'

The woman behind her emitted a frightened squeak before being shushed by her travelling companion.

Amy ignored them, too intent on watching the confidence slip from her quarry's face.

'Whereas you,' she continued, 'bear an uncanny resemblance to Taylor King, a drug dealer wanted in two States with an Interpol fan club demanding his extradition to France.'

King muttered under his breath, sagging further into his seat.

Amy smirked. 'Your mistake was leaving a trail from the boat ramp to the plane, including the gun you dumped in the smoking area outside the airport. What were you hoping to do, King – try to leave the country by boat once you got here?'

He mumbled something in response.

'I didn't catch that, King – speak up,' Amy said, ignoring the ruckus behind her as the exit door opened and three armed tactical officers stormed into the cabin.

'Vanuatu,' said King. He lowered his sleeve, glaring at her through red-rimmed eyes.

Amy frowned and reached into the backpack once more.

A chill shivered down her spine as her fingers touched hard plastic, and she pulled out a 3D printed gun.

King glowered at her. 'And I would have made it there without you.'

# CHAPTER SIX

Amy was bundled from the aircraft behind Taylor King, surrounded by armed men in bulky black bulletproof vests and carrying semi-automatic rifles.

In their wake, a cabin full of shocked passengers exploded with noise, demanding explanations and a hasty exit off the plane before her shoes touched the metal staircase and their voices faded away.

She reached the bottom of the stairs and watched while King was bundled into an armoured police vehicle and then whisked away, sirens blaring.

'Sergeant Cornish.'

She turned to see a burly man in his fifties approaching, and took a step backwards despite the pips on his shoulder epaulettes. 'Commander Granger.'

Confusion swept through her, and then she saw the familiar logo of a national television news channel emblazoned down the side of a van that was barrelling towards them.

'I hope they're not expecting to speak to me, sir.'

'Not at all. Come this way. Can I take that bag for you?'

'I'm fine, thanks.' Amy shifted the strap across her shoulder and glanced towards the plane. 'I need to be with my family. I need—'

'In a moment. Over here.' He steered her towards the shade of the hangar. 'Did King give any indication why he was flying up here after he killed McIntyre?'

'He said he was meeting some friends, and that one of them had a boat.'

'Right, okay. I'll have someone liaise with the city harbour patrol and send a couple of cars down to the marina. If he was meeting someone, we might still catch them before they realise he's not turning up.'

'Why didn't you arrest him before he boarded the flight, sir? Surely it would've been safer than this.'

'We didn't have a choice – King might've taken hostages given half the chance. If he did that, he could've got the pilot to take him anywhere he wanted and we wouldn't have been able to stop him. At least now we can interview him here and find out who his accomplices are. He might be willing to talk given that he was walking around with McIntyre's shirt.' Granger squinted against the bright sunlight streaming through the hangar door, and beckoned to one of his superintendents before turning back to Amy. 'We'll do a full debrief at district headquarters downtown at five o'clock but I'll let you get back to your family for now.'

'Thanks,' she managed. She handed him the Glock. 'And you can have this. I'm meant to be on holiday.'

Granger's eyes narrowed. 'You were the only one close enough at short notice.'

'That's what you said last time. You went too far today, sir. You put my family in danger.'

'We didn't.' He jerked his head towards the line of passengers disembarking from the aeroplane, their necks craning while they tried to catch a glimpse of what was taking place inside the hangar. 'They and everyone else on board that flight was safe, because of *you*. Thanks to you, we have one of Australia's biggest drug smugglers in custody.'

She glared up at him, met a steely gaze in response, and bit her lip.

'Sir, did you know that Taylor smuggled a 3D printed weapon through security?'

He paled beneath his brusque demeanour, then rubbed his chin. 'No. No, we didn't. Where is it now?'

'One of the armed response team took it into evidence with the shirt.' Amy crossed her arms while the commander squirmed.

'There'll be a full inquiry, of course.' Granger cleared his throat, pausing to inspect a large diving watch. 'But for now, you've got four hours until the debrief. We've arranged for a car to take you and your family to your hotel, and I'll send someone to collect you later. Don't be late.'

He turned, not waiting for her response, and evidently not expecting one.

Amy leaned against the hangar door, her legs shaking while the adrenalin ebbed away.

The aircraft was abandoned now, the crew standing behind Commander Granger while he addressed a swelling group of journalists.

Passengers crowded towards the three

buses approaching from the terminal, their heads bowed while they updated their social media, simultaneously marking themselves as "safe" while sharing their version of events, and eyeing the business class passengers with ill-disguised envy.

She shook her head in disgust, then spotted the man and the toddler walking towards her and smiled, relief feathering the first tentative acceptance of a job well done.

'Jesus, Morgan, am I glad to see you.'

'Mummy!'

'Oh my God, Carrie.' Amy swept the little girl into her arms as Morgan's arms wrapped around her shoulders.

The toddler pouted. 'Daddy called me Lizzy.'

'I'm sorry – she was off and running before I could stop her,' he murmured. 'I was so scared. When I saw him… All I could think of was for Chrissakes make up a name—'

'It's okay, don't worry. I'm safe, we're all safe.' She snuggled into his chest, clawing at his cotton shirt. 'It's done.'

'Until next time.' Morgan's face clouded.

'There won't be a next time. I'm quitting, as of now.'

He raised an eyebrow. 'Does Granger know?'

'Not yet.'

'Mummy, can we go snorkelling?'

Amy turned and buried her nose into her daughter's hair, the faint scent of mandarin shampoo enveloping her. 'We can do whatever you want to do, Carrie.'

Reaching out for Morgan, she wrapped her fingers around his and squeezed.

'Well done, love.' He grinned. 'And there was you telling me all these years that you're scared of flying.'

Amy managed a smile as she lowered Carrie to the ground.

'I wasn't lying about that,' she said, then swung Taylor King's backpack over her shoulder, tested the weight of the bundles of cash that shifted inside, and wondered how long it would take them to sail from Port Douglas to Vanuatu.


THE END

# ABOUT THE AUTHOR

Rachel Amphlett is a USA Today bestselling author of crime fiction and spy thrillers, many of which have been translated worldwide.

Her novels are available in eBook, print, and audiobook formats from libraries and retailers as well as her website shop.

A keen traveller, Rachel has both Australian and British citizenship.

Find out more about Rachel's books at: www.rachelamphlett.com.

Blood on Snow

A suburban housewife is found dead in her garden. There is no weapon, no witnesses, and the only set of footprints belong to her cat.

Probationary detective Kay Hunter and her colleagues are convinced it's murder – but how can they find a killer when there are no clues?

ISBN eBook: 978-1-913498-70-2
ISBN paperback: 978-1-913498-71-9

The Reckoning

The newest arrival at a care home for the elderly carries an air of mystery that even an ex-WW2 Resistance fighter can't help trying to solve.

Then matters take a sinister turn…

ISBN eBook: 978-1-913498-70-2
ISBN paperback: 978-1-913498-71-9

Staying at a tiny guesthouse in Cornwall after the summer, Julie spends her days combing the beaches, looking for things to collect while hiding from her past.

Then a storm breaks, and suddenly she's scared.

**Because you never know what might wash up after a storm…**

ISBN eBook: 978-1-913498-93-1
ISBN paperback: 978-1-913498-94-8

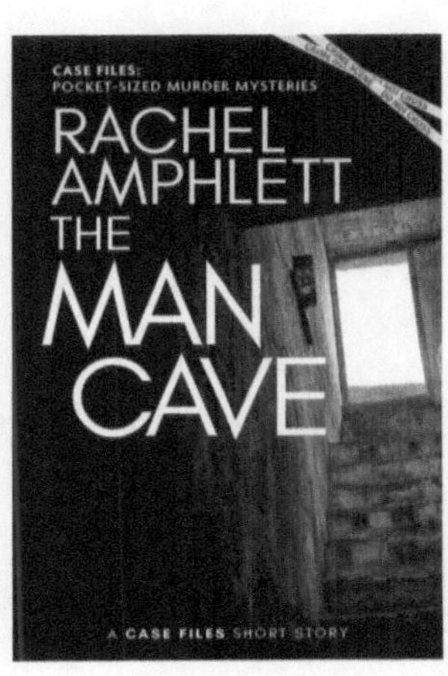

The Man Cave

When Darren regains consciousness in a dank basement, escape turns out to be the least of his worries...

ISBN eBook: 978-1-913498-96-2
ISBN paperback: 978-1-913498-97-9